IN A CERTAIN LAND

Wise Fools, Cunning Dragons, and Baba Yaga

NICHOLAS KOTAR

WAYSTONE

PRESS

In a Certain Land

Wise Fools, Cunning Dragons, and Baba Yaga

Translated and retold by
Nicholas Kotar

Cover design and interior art by Ewan Craig

Interior design and editing by Katherine Hyde

❀ Created with Vellum

INTRODUCTION

Dr. Martin Shaw, author of Bardskull

Nicholas Kotar is doing us all service by retelling these wonderful stories. Hidden away are all sorts of secrets about how to live: under the wing of a story is often where ancestral wisdoms are placed. They hide in plain sight, not regarded as important as philosophy or some other strangulated artform. Why? Because they speak to all ages. They transmit their genius through image and narrative. Indeed a six-year-old could sit next to a grandmother and both be edified by the same tale. If the story can't speak to the mind of a six-year-old it's likely not a fairy tale; if it doesn't hold enough complexity for an adult it's likely not a fairy tale either. That wing I mentioned is broad, and covers all.

Fairy tales tend to show not tell. A storyteller lets the images do the work and the imagination of the reader do the meaning-making. If you theorise as you go, you likely commit murder to the thing you are trying to honour. It gets weighed down with allegory; it simply becomes a vehicle for a polemical moral tale. Fairy tales are wilder than that. More unruly. Mercifully Nicholas favours a rather old-world approach. As I've often said, don't tell the story what it is; it may mean something else next time.

When the world is no longer making sense, go to the fairy tales. Not some vast and multifaceted myth, but just a humble tale. It will be waiting for you, just where you left it. It has what you need. There will be firebird feathers and whirling chicken huts, there will be horses that can speak and brothers that betray. It is a thrilling and layered world you are entering. It is the imagination of your great-great-great-great-great grandparents you are contacting, and more beside. You will learn as much from Kotar's tales as you will from a DNA test, regardless of where you were born.

IVAN THE PEASANT'S SON
AND THE DRAGONISH
MONSTER

In a certain kingdom, in a certain land, there lived an old man and an old woman, and they had three sons. The youngest was called Ivan. They lived well, were never lazy, constantly working at sowing and reaping, and they had more than enough to live on.

But a terrible rumor began to spread in that country. A horrible dragonish monster was planning on invading their land, to destroy all the people, to burn down to the ground all the villages and towns. The old man and woman grew sorrowful at this turn of events. But their elder sons sought to comfort them:

"Don't sorrow, dear mother and father, we will go in battle against the dragonish monster, we will fight it and kill it dead. But we don't want you to worry too much, so we'll leave Ivanushka here with you. He's too young to go to war."

"What's that?" complained Ivan. "I have no intention of staying behind my mother's skirts and waiting around, sucking my thumb. I'm coming along to fight the dragonish monster!"

The old man and woman wouldn't dream of trying to persuade Ivan otherwise. They prepared all three of their sons for the journey. The brothers took their swords, a bundle of bread and salt, sat on their horses, and rode away.

They rode and they rode, and arrived at some distant village. All around: not a single living soul to be seen, everything's burned down, broken, all save a single little hut.

The brothers entered that hut. Inside, they found an old woman lying on the shelf of the stove, moaning and groaning her grief.

"Hello, grandmother!" said the brothers.

"Good day, my fine fellows. Where are you off to?"

"We are on our way to the river Currant, to the arrow-wood bridge. We want to fight the dragonish monster, to stop it from coming into our lands."

"Oh, my fine fellows! What a good deed this is! For that dragonish monster has destroyed everything in sight, stolen all the fine things, left no one alive. Now he has reached our own lands, and I'm the last one living. It seems I'm too stringy for the dragonish monster to munch on."

The brothers spent the night at the old woman's hut, and in the early morning they got up and were once again on the road.

They reached the Currant River and saw the arrow-wood bridge still standing. All along the banks of that river lay strewn broken bows and arrows and rusted swords, and next to them the bones of dead warriors shone dully in the waning sunlight.

The brothers found an empty hut and decided to stay the night there.

"Well, brothers," said Ivan, "we've come to a foreign land. We must listen to everything, keep an eye out for everything. Let's take turns staying awake at night, lest the dragonish monster come over the bridge at night."

The first night, the eldest stood guard. He walked along the banks of the Currant, but everything was still as can be; no one walked or skulked in the shadows, nothing made a sound.

So the eldest brother lay down in the brush and fell asleep so deeply, he snored.

But Ivan lies awake in the hut, his eyes wide and worried. When it struck past midnight, he rose and put on his sword. There he saw (and heard) his brother sleeping, snoring as only a brave warrior can.

But Ivan didn't wake him; instead he hid under the arrowwood bridge and waited.

Suddenly the river-water boiled, the eagles on the oak branches screamed, and the dragonish monster came riding up on its horse, all six heads intent on the bridge. He mounted the bridge and crested its peak, when his horse tripped, the black raven on his shoulder croaked, and the black dog behind him growled.

The dragonish monster with the six heads said, "Why, O horse of mine, did you trip? Why, black raven of mine, did you croak? Why, black dog of mine, did you growl? Or do you sense that Ivan, the peasant's son, is somewhere near? But he can't have been born yet, and if he has, he's still a boy! No good for battle. I'll put him in one palm, and I'll swat him like a fly with the other."

But then Ivan, the peasant's son, came out from under the bridge and said, "Don't boast, you foul dragonish monster. You didn't shoot the bright falcon down from the sky; it's too early to start plucking out his feathers. You don't recognize this warrior; no point in shaming me. Let's instead test our strength. Whoever wins, he'll be the boaster!"

And they did. They fell on each other with such fury that the ground itself groaned from the strain.

The dragonish monster had no fortune that day. With a single blow, Ivan chopped off three of its heads.

"Hold, Ivan, son of a peasant," exclaimed the monster. "Give me a moment to catch my breath!"

"What rest? You have three heads, dragon, and I have one! When you have one left, then we can take a break."

But with a single blow Ivan chopped off the remaining three heads as well. He chopped the body of the dragonish monster into little pieces, threw them into the Currant River, and put the six heads under the bridge. After he was done, he went back to the hut and lay down to sleep.

In the morning, the eldest brother came home. Ivan asked him, "Well, brother, did you see anything?"

"No, brother! Not a single fly flew by my head all night."

Ivan answered him not a word.

The next night, it was the middle son's turn to watch. He walked around for a while, looked in all four directions, and stopped worrying. He climbed into a bush and fell asleep.

Ivan had no trust in his middle brother either.

When it struck past midnight, he rose and put on his sword. There he saw (and heard) his brother sleeping, snoring as only a brave warrior can.

But Ivan didn't wake him; instead he hid under the arrow-wood bridge and waited.

Suddenly the river-water boiled, the eagles on the oak branches screamed, and the dragonish monster came riding up on his horse, all nine of his heads intent on the bridge. He mounted the bridge and crested its peak, when his horse tripped, the black raven on his shoulder croaked, and the black dog behind him growled.

The dragonish monster with the nine heads said, "Why, O horse of mine, did you trip? Why, black raven of mine, did you croak? Why, black dog of mine, did you growl? Or do you sense that Ivan, the peasant's son, is somewhere near? But he can't have been born yet, and if he has, he's still a boy! No good for battle. I'll crush him with my finger."

But then Ivan, the peasant's son, came out from under the bridge and said, "Don't boast, you foul dragonish monster, before you've finished the job. We'll see who wins!"

Ivan swung his sharp sword, and with a single blow, three heads fell a-tumblin'. But the dragonish monster struck Ivan, and he drove him knee-deep into the ground. Ivan took a handful of sand and threw it into the face of the beast. While the monster wiped his weeping eyes, Ivan took two swings of his sword. And all six heads fell tumbling down. Ivan chopped the monster into pieces, threw them into the river, and laid the nine heads under the bridge. Then he returned to the hut and lay down to sleep, as though nothing at all had happened.

In the morning, the middle brother returned.

"Well," said Ivan. "Anything to report, dear brother of mine?"

"No, I saw nothing. Not a single fly flew by my head, not even a mosquito whined near to my ear!"

"Well, if that's the case," said Ivan, "come with me, my brothers dear! I'll show you both a fly and a mosquito!"

He brought them to the arrow-wood bridge, and he showed them the heads of the monsters.

"Look at the size of the flies and mosquitoes that fly around these parts at night!" he said.

And the brothers, they were ashamed.

"We were so tired," they both said in unison.

On the third night, Ivan himself went to watch.

He said to his brothers, "I'm going to a wage a battle fell. Don't sleep, my dears, but listen carefully. When you hear me whistling, then untie my horse, and come yourselves to my aid."

Ivan the peasant's son came to the Currant River, and he hid under the bridge, and he waited.

No sooner did midnight strike than the ground itself began to shake, the waters boiled, the winds howled, and the eagles on the oaks screamed their terror. A dragonish monster with twelve heads rode on a steed up to the bridge. All twelve heads were shrieking, all twelve heads simmered with fire in the gorge. The horse of that beast had twelve wings, its hide was of iron, and its tail was of steel. No sooner did that monstrous steed set foot on the wood of the arrow-wood bridge than it tripped. The black raven on the monster's shoulder croaked, and the black dog behind him growled. The dragonish monster beat his horse with a whip, then his raven and his dog for good measure.

"Why, my steed, did you trip over your own hooves? Why, black raven, did you croak? Why, black dog, did you growl just now? Can it be that Ivan, the peasant's son, is here? Impossible! He's not born yet, and even if he is, he's too small to battle the likes of me. I'll just breathe on him, and there won't even be any ashes left of his body."

Then Ivan, the peasant's son, came up from under the bridge, and he said, "Enough boasting, you beast. You'll embarrass yourself!"

"So it is you, Ivan, you son of a peasant! Why have you come here? To die?"

"I've come to look at your power, my foe! I've come to test your strength."

"Who are you to test my strength? You're a fly before me!"

And then Ivan answered, "I came not to tell you fairy tales, nor to listen to yours. I came to fight you to the death, and to save the good people from you!"

Ivan swung his sharp sword, and three heads of the monster he struck off. But the dragonish monster raised up its own heads, wiped them with his fiery finger, and put them back on their stumps. And they grew back as though they had never fallen off!

Thing were going badly for Ivan. With his shriek the monster deafened him, with his fire he burned him, with his sparks he showered him, and he dug him into the ground to the knees with a blow.

But he couldn't help snickering, too. "Maybe you'd like to take a break, Ivan, you son of a peasant?"

"What? No rest for the wicked. Come at me, you beast!"

Ivan whistled, Ivan called, he threw his gauntlet into the

hut. The gauntlet broke the window, but all Ivan heard from that hole was their snores.

Ivan gathered his strength, swung his mighty sword, and six heads came off at a blow. But the dragonish monster just picked them up and put them right back on his shoulders. He struck Ivan a mighty blow, and Ivan was buried to his waist.

Ivan could see that things were not going well. He took off his left gauntlet and threw it at the hut. The gauntlet broke the roof of the hut, but the brothers kept sleeping, and they heard not a thing.

A third time Ivan gathered all his strength and struck the dragonish monster a mighty blow. Nine heads came flying off, but the monster just took them, traced them with his fiery finger, and they grew right back. He fell upon Ivan and buried him to his shoulders.

Ivan took off his hat and threw it at the hut. From that blow, the hut shuddered to its foundations, and only then did the brothers come awake, and they listened. They heard: Ivan's horse was neighing to high heaven.

They opened the stable, they untied the horse, and they came to Ivanushka's aid themselves.

The horse rode up, attacked the beast with its hooves, tore at it with its teeth. But the dragonish monster shrieked and screamed, and showered the horse with his sparks.

By that time, Ivan had dug himself out, and he struck the dragonish monster on the hand! The fiery finger he chopped right off, and then began hacking at the heads. All of them he lopped off, then he chopped the beast up and threw the pieces into the river.

And only then did the brothers arrive to help.

"You sleepyheads!" he cried at them. "Your dreaming nearly cost me my head!"

The abashed brothers brought him home to the hut. Then they washed him, fed him, and put him to sleep.

Early in the morning, Ivan was up with the sun, and already he was putting on his boots.

"Where are you going so early, Ivan? You should rest after such a terrible battle!"

"No," answered Ivan, "there's no time to rest. I lost my belt somewhere near the river. I must find it."

"What a fool," said his brothers. "Why not go into town and buy yourself a new one?"

"No, I need my own!" said Ivan.

And he went, but not to search for his belt. Instead, he crossed over the Currant River and crept into the fiery palace of the monster.

In that palace he saw three dragonish brides and their mother, the old, canny serpent.

They sat together, and they plotted and planned.

The first one said, "I will pay back Ivan. I will catch him unawares as he travels home with his brothers. I will send a great heat on them, then I'll turn into a well. When they come to me to drink my water, I'll swallow them whole!"

The old serpent mother approved of this plan.

Then the second bride said, "I will hurry ahead of them and turn into an apple tree. If they reach for my fine-looking apples and eat them, they'll be torn apart from the inside."

"Oh, what an excellent plan," said the serpent-mother.

And the third of the dragonish brides then said, "I will send on them a magical sleep, then I'll rush on ahead of them and turn into a carpet with comfortable silken pillows. The brothers will want nothing more than to rest, but as soon as they lie down, they'll be burned up in flame!"

"And you've come up with a great one as well," hissed the mother, that canniest serpent. "But if you all fail, my daughters-in-law, then I myself will come upon them and swallow them whole."

Ivan heard it all, then returned to his brothers.

"Well, Ivanushka, did you find your belt?"

"Oh, I did indeed."

"What a waste of time!"

"Not at all, my dear brothers!"

But he said no more than that.

Then all three of the brothers gathered their things and rode on back to their home.

They rode through the fields, they rode through the meadows. But the day was so hot and so dry that their thirst was unbearable. Suddenly, they saw a well by the road, and inside that well was a silver cup. The brothers said to Ivan, "Let's stop, Ivanushka, let's drink our fill."

Ivan answered, "But who knows what sort of water that is? What if it's dirty or poisoned?"

And he jumped from his horse and unsheathed his sword. He attacked that well as though it were an enemy. The well wailed, roared in a horrible voice. Then, suddenly, a fog appeared out of nowhere. The heat disappeared, and with it their thirst.

"See, my brothers, what sort of water that well had!"

"Oh, we see, Ivanushka," they answered.

They rode on, who knows how long. Suddenly they saw an apple tree in the field. The apples on that tree were pink and juicy.

The brothers jumped off their horses and reached for the fruits, but Ivanushka outran them and hacked at the tree until nothing was left but the roots.

The apple tree wailed, the apple tree screamed.

"Look, my brothers, what tasty apples this tree has!"

And they rode on away from that terrible place. They rode for a long time until exhaustion overtook them. And look! Just ahead of them, there's a comfortable rug with plushy pillows covered in silk!

"Oh, let's take a small break, Ivanushka, let's sleep on these pillows. Just an hour, no more."

"No, brothers, there won't be any comfort on those pillows!"

But the brothers grew angry with Ivan this time.

"Who made you our leader, to tell us what to do. We have our own good sense!"

And Ivanushka answered them not a single word. Instead, he took off his belt and threw it on the rug. In an instant the belt exploded in flames, until there was nothing left at all.

"That's what would have happened to you, my dear brothers!"

Ivan unsheathed his sword and attacked the rug as though it were a warrior in battle. He chopped it into little pieces and said, "Pointless was your rebuke, my brothers. The well and the tree and the rug, they're not what they seem. Each of them was a dragonish wife. They wanted to kill us, but instead they got what they deserved."

The brothers rode on until the sky grew black, the winds howled, and the ground itself groaned. Behind them flew the old serpent-mother. She opened her maw from the sky to the ground; she wanted to swallow them whole. But the young men, no fools they, threw their packets of bread and salt into her mouth. The serpent was thrilled—she thought that she'd captured the three brothers in her mouth. She stopped and she chewed. But there was nothing but salt. So she spat it out and flew back in pursuit.

Ivan can see that his time is up, and he pushed his horse to the limits of its speed. They rode and they rode, and look! A smithy on the side of the road with twelve smiths beating their anvils.

"Smiths, smiths, let us into your smithy!"

And they did. Then they closed the twelve iron doors and locked them with twelve iron locks.

The serpent-mother flew up to that smithy.

"Smiths, smiths, give me Ivan the peasant's son and his brothers!"

But the smiths answered her, "Lick the twelve iron doors with your tongue, and you'll have them!"

The dragon mother began licking the doors. She licked and she licked, and eleven doors she melted. One final door remained in her way.

But she was exhausted, and she sat down to rest. At that moment, Ivan, the peasant's son, jumped out of the smithy and grabbed the serpent-mother. With all his might, he drove her head into the rocks. And she fell apart into ashes and dust, and the wind carried that dust away. From that day forward, no serpents or dragonish monsters remained. The people began to live without fear again.

And Ivan the peasant's son returned home with his brothers. And they lived on as they had, plowing the field, sowing the ground, and reaping its rewards.

THE POOR MAN AND HIS THREE SONS

Once there lived a poor man who had three sons. The eldest was called Dimitri, the second Andrei, and the youngest Ivan.

When the boys had grown up, the father called them to his side and said:

"I'm old and tired, my children, and I can no longer take care of you. You're old enough to go out into the world and fend for yourselves. I'll be expecting you back in a year's time. The one who has earned the most will stay with me to the end of my days."

The sons left home, and soon each found himself some work.

After a year, the eldest son returned with lots of money; the next day the second son arrived with a bag of gold; and the next day after that, the youngest son came home with nothing at all.

The father was furious with him and kicked him out of their home.

Poor Ivanushka had nothing left to do but go. For days on end, he walked and he walked. He entered a wild, slumbering forest, sat down on a stump, looked at the last crust of bread he had brought from home. What else could he do? He began to weep, chewing at the hard lump of old bread. And so absorbed was he in his own sorrow that he didn't see a giant come up right in front of him.

"Why are you crying, my boy?" asked the giant.

Ivan looked at him for a moment, shrugged his shoulders, and told him everything.

"Well, that is quite a sad story," said the giant. "If you like, you can come work for me?"

Ivan agreed. He and his new master walked to the very heart of that dark forest. There, the giant had built a snug cottage for his home. Well, it was snug for a giant, so there was plenty of room for Ivan!

He lived well. There was not much work to do. The giant taught him how to ride a horse and how to wield a sword. He also taught Ivan how to read, how to write, and how to count. And there were other, deeper things that Ivan learned by watching and waiting and not asking too many questions.

A year passed in this manner. Then, one day the giant came home and said:

"Ivan, it is time for you to test your mettle. Saddle your horse, take your sword, and ride south. There, beyond two mountains, you will find a black castle protected by a black wall. In this castle lives a black *upyr* whom you must destroy."

Ivan had heard of the upyri before; all boys had. They were monsters that sucked the life out of you. Nightmares come true.

But Ivan still prepared for the journey, said goodbye to his benefactor, and rode south.

At last, after riding for three days, he saw the black castle protected by a black wall. Ivan made his way into the court-yard, and there he saw the upyr sitting on an iron throne with an iron club in his hands.

The upyr demanded in a horrible voice:

"What do you want with me? How dare you walk upon my land?"

"I've come to test my mettle against you, monster!" replied Ivan.

The upyr roared with hideous laughter and hurled the iron club at Ivan. He missed. Then Ivan picked it up, swung it, and struck the upyr so hard that the monster dropped dead. Ivan entered the black castle and found a black horse in black harness there. He jumped on the black horse, tied his own horse to the black's saddle, and rode home.

The giant had been waiting anxiously for Ivanushka. When he saw him come back on the black horse, he was thrilled and praised him to the skies.

Some time passed. With every day, Ivan grew wiser and stronger. Another fine day came when the giant called him and said:

"Now you must ride north, Ivanushka. When you pass through the slumbering forest and the impassable swamp, you will see a castle of red stone, protected by a red wall. In that castle lives a red upyr who has long harried the people of that land. You must kill him."

Ivan wasted no time and rode north on that very same day.

He rode and rode until he came upon a wild, dark forest. He could hardly make his way through on horseback, so he unsheathed his sword and hacked a path for himself. He slashed and he cut until the moon rose in the starlit sky. He broke camp and hobbled his horse, lest it should stray away. Then Ivan lay down on the springy moss under an oak tree and was soon fast asleep.

But something disturbed his sleep. There was a kind of music in the air, and when he woke up, he saw that the trees around him had moved. He was in a clearing inside the forest that glowed with a beautiful light, and the ground was carpeted with flowers. In the trees birds were singing more beautifully than Ivan had ever heard before.

Attracted by the sounds, the *vila* came out of the forest and the *vodyanie* crawled out of the lakes to dance and sing together. All the animals of the forest gathered around them, the wolves sitting together with the fawns. On a creaky branch above Ivan's head, a dove snuggled with an old owl. The owl was telling her stories, and the dove listened attentively.

Ivan, too, listened in on the owl's story. And this is what he heard: This forest was a cursed forest, and all the creatures in it had died. But Ivan's clearing of the road had brought everyone back to life. This was why the birds and animals and spirits were so joyful.

Ivan looked with wonder at this forest scene, and when he awoke again the next morning, he was not sure if what he had seen was real or a dream. Awakening at dawn, he saw that he was on the very edge of that forest, bordering a great field covered with flowers.

The swamps have already dried up, he thought. *It is time to destroy the upyr.*

Ivan mounted his horse and galloped away. Not long after, he saw the red castle protected by a wall of red stones. He rode into the courtyard. Once again, on an iron throne sat the upyr, red as blood, clutching a club twice the size of Ivan himself.

They started to fight. The upyr was soon drained of his strength, and Ivan finished him off. Inside the castle, he found a red horse in red harness. He jumped on it and tied his own horse to the red saddle. Then he rode home.

On his way, he saw people in the fields, plowing and haying already. Ivan felt joy at the sight and hurried on home to tell the giant what had happened. His master was overjoyed to see Ivan safe and sound. He took the horse and harness, and Ivanushka went to bed for a good, long rest.

But Ivan's rest was cut short, because the giant called him to himself one final time. He told him to ride east, for there lived a white upyr. This time, Ivanushka rode through arid steppes and hot deserts. Huge dragons tried to eat him. Monstrous spiders attacked him, trying to tie him up in their webs. At night, as he slept, nightmares seemed to come alive to frighten him from his path. It was a country of phantoms and ghosts, where even lakes and rivers moved away from him when he approached, trying to slake his terrible thirst.

Through it all, Ivan stubbornly kept to the road, and at last he came to a huge white castle protected by a wall of white stones. The white upyr was the most fearsome of them all. For three days and nights, Ivan fought him. In the end, he killed the white upyr, took away his white horse and harness, and rushed back home.

As he rode, Ivan saw that the arid steppes were covered in flowers. The empty deserts had turned into forests. Brooks bubbled in deep gullies, lakes sparkled in the midday sun, and birds sang their songs in the trees.

Ivan came home, gave the horse and harness to the giant, and went to rest.

He lived with the giant for a time after that, always learning, always watching, always growing wiser and stronger.

But all this time the question nagged at him: Why did the giant, who was far stronger than Ivan, not go and slay the upyri himself?

Finally, he could no longer restrain the question. And he asked:

"My dear master and friend, for years I have not asked anything of you. And so don't begrudge me a question at last. Why did not you, so strong as you are, go and kill the monsters yourself?"

The giant smiled and answered:

"Ah, Ivanushka, what a question! Listen then to my words: When a great deed is performed by a strong man, it is no great thing. But when the deeds of the strong are accomplished by the weak and young—that is a very great thing indeed! Now hear this advice from me, for you have grown great indeed. Great deeds are often performed not by the wise and the strong of body, but by those who are strong in will and desire."

Finally, the giant himself went on a journey, and Ivan came with him. They rode many days, finally passing through a city that was deathly quiet. Black flags drooped from the flagpoles. Ivan asked an old man, "Tell me, what evil has befallen this city?"

The old man answered, "Our city has attracted the notice of a great dragon. He has demanded gifts of cattle, and all our stores are empty. But even this is not enough. Now he demands that we bring him the daughter of the king! She has a good heart and has agreed to give herself up to the monster willingly. That's why this city is grieving. If only there were someone brave enough to stand before that dragon, I'm sure the king would do anything for him! Even give him his daughter in marriage."

The giant looked for a long time at his servant.

"Ivanushka, it is time. You must free the king's daughter and rescue this land from the monster."

But first, they returned home. Ivanushka untied the black horse he had taken from the black upyr, bade farewell to the giant, and set off for the city.

When he arrived there, he was too late: the king's daughter had already given herself to the dragon, and the monster had just taken her to his lair in the forest. Ivan overtook the dragon just as he was approaching the opening of a large cave.

"'Princess!" Ivan cried out. "It's too early for you to die!"

When she saw Ivan, the tears on her cheeks dried up and she smiled at him with eyes filled with joy. The dragon, recognizing the black horse of the dead upyr, crawled into its cave to hide. Ivan ran to the cave and cried out:

"Hey, you! Come out of there, or are you too scared to fight a bug like myself?!"

Hissing angrily, the dragon flew out of the cave with his

talons bared. Ivan jumped on his horse and unsheathed his sword.

They clashed and fought like lightning and thunder. Ivan chopped one head after another off the dragon's body. But no sooner did one head fall than another appeared in its place, spitting fire at Ivan. Soon Ivan felt his strength pouring out of him.

Finally, the dragon knocked him and his horse to the ground, landed on Ivan, and opened its great jaws to eat him alive. With a final thrust, Ivan ripped open the monster's belly. The dragon let out a roar that shook the leaves off the trees. But it was the final cry of the beast.

Ivan looked about him and saw the princess standing at a distance.

"Why are you so sad, princess? The dragon is dead. You can go home to your parents," he said to her.

"I don't want to go home alone," she said. "Come with me, for you have saved me and my people."

She took Ivan by the hand, and they mounted his horse and rode.

In the city, the banner still drooped and the people still wept and wailed at the loss of their beloved princess and the foolish champion who had come too late to save her.

"Stop crying, I'm alive," she cried. "Ivan has rescued me!"

What a cheer there was at her words! The people thronged after them to the king's palace. When the king saw her beaming with happiness, he wept for joy. When he was told that Ivan had saved his daughter from certain death, he gave her in marriage to him.

And then they feasted their wedding for seven whole days! I was there too, you know, drinking all the wine and mead, but it all poured off my mustaches and not into my mouth!

THE TALE OF BABA YAGA

In a certain kingdom, in a certain land, there lived a peasant with his wife. They had twin children—a son and a daughter. One day the wife died. Her husband loved her dearly, and he mourned over her for a very long time. A year passed, then two years, and even more years than that. But facts are facts: a house with no woman is a house with no harmony. So a day came when the man thought, "Perhaps I should marry again."

He did, and he even had children from his second wife.

The stepmother was envious of her stepson and daughter and began to use them terribly. She attacked them at the slightest provocation, sent them outside whenever she could. She took the best of her food for her own children but left the leavings for the others.

In her heart of hearts, she wanted to get rid of them.

An evil thought had appeared in the heart of the stepmother. At first she only nursed it quietly in the evenings, but soon it consumed her attention even in the broad daylight. She decided to send the children to Baba Yaga, thinking for certain that they would never come back from that terrible place.

"Dear children," she said to the orphans one day, "you must

go to my grandmother who lives in the forest. I have long neglected her, and you must do your duty as children. She is an odd creature, but if you do what she tells you—everything, mind you—she will give you sweet rolls and honey and send you on home."

The orphans went. But the sister—she was sharp as a tack, that one!—took her brother by the hand and instead ran to their own father's old, old grandmother and told her all about this trip to the forest.

"Oh, my poor dear!" said the good old grandmother. "My heart aches for you. That is no sweet old grandmother you go to visit but Baba Yaga herself! Now listen to me, my darlings, and pay heed to my words. I will give you the only help I can. Be kind and good to everyone you meet; do not speak unkind words to anyone; do not despise those who are weakest, and never forget that unlooked-for help always comes at the darkest hour."

The old, old grandmother gave the children some milk to drink and to each a slice of meat. She gave them some sweet bread-rolls to boot, and when the children departed, she stood watching them a long, long time.

The children entered the slumbering forest and—oh, what a sight!—there stood a hut on chicken's feet, spinning round and round about itself. The girl mustered her courage and cried out, "Hut! Hut! Turn around with your back to the forest and your door to me!"

The hut listened, and the door opened on its own. The orphans looked inside the open door and saw Baba Yaga lying on top of the stove, one foot in one corner, the other in another, her bony knees sticking to the rafters.

"Foo, foo, foo!" cried Baba Yaga. "Who brought that Russian stink here?"

The children were afraid and stood very close together, but still they said, remembering their old, old grandmother,

"Hello, grandmother, our stepmother sent us to help you around the house."

"Oh, did she, my pretties? Very well, very well. You can stay for a bit. Do everything I say, and I'll feed and clothe you. But if you don't, I'll eat you!"

Immediately, the witch ordered the girl to spin thread. The boy she commanded to fill a tub of water with nothing but a sieve! The poor orphan girl wept at her spinning-wheel and wiped away her bitter tears. Suddenly, a grey mouse appeared out of nowhere.

"Little girl, don't cry. Give me something to eat and I'll help you."

The little girl pulled out a piece of her sweet bread-roll and gave it to the mouse.

The mouse ate its fill and seemed quite the better for it.

"Now," squeaked the mouse, "go and find the black cat. He is very hungry (he's been trying to eat me for years, no luck!). Give him a bit of meat, and he will help you."

The girl went in search of the cat and saw her brother in great distress about the tub. He had filled the sieve many times, yet the tub was still dry. Two little birds passed by and sang to the children: "Kind little children, give us some crumbs and we will help you."

The orphans did so.

"Clay and water, dear children!" sang the birds, and away they flew through the air.

The girl immediately understood, spat in the sieve, plastered it up with clay, and filled the tub in no time at all. Then they returned to the hut and saw the black cat lounging at the door. They gave him the best piece of the meat their old granny had given them.

"Dear cat, so black and beautiful, tell us how to get away from Baba Yaga."

"Well," answered the cat very seriously, "since you gave me the best piece of meat, I will help you. Here is a towel and a comb. Take these and run away as fast as you can. When you hear the witch running after you, drop the towel behind your back. If you hear her once again, then throw down the comb."

Just at that moment, Baba Yaga came home. She looked quite disheartened that the children had done so well.

"Well," she complained into her hook of a nose, "today you were brave and smart; but we'll see about tomorrow. Your work won't be so easy this time. I'm pretty sure I'll be having you for dinner this time."

The poor orphans went to bed on a pallet of straw in a cold corner. The next morning, even before the sun came up, the children took the towel and comb and ran away as fast as their feet could carry them.

Immediately, the dogs were after them, but they threw them the rest of their grandmother's scraps. The gates refused to budge, but the children smoothed them with oil and they screeched open. The birch tree near the path reached out to scratch their eyes, but the girl fastened her own prettiest ribbon to it. So they went farther and farther and ran out of the slumbering forest back into the fields of grass and wheat.

Meanwhile, the cat sat down by the loom and tore the girl's thread to pieces with great gusto.

Baba Yaga returned. "Where are the children?" she yelled as she beat the cat. "Why have you let them go, you traitor? You were supposed to scratch their faces!"

The cat answered, "I served you for years and years and years, and not once did you ever give me anything tasty. Those sweet children gave me some excellent meat."

The witch screamed at the dogs, the gates, and the birch tree near the path.

"Well," barked the dogs, "you may be our master, but you've not been very nice at all, and the orphans were kind to us."

The gates replied, "We listen to you always, but look at us, we're nothing but rotten wood and rusted hinges, and the children smoothed us with oil."

The birch tree lisped with its leaves, "Look at this pretty ribbon."

Baba Yaga bellowed and ran after the children herself. She jumped into a huge mortar, pushed off with her huge pestle, and flew away away away into the sky!

The children heard her coming and threw the towel behind them. At once a river appeared in the middle of the field. Baba Yaga hopped along the shore back and forth, back and forth, until she pushed down her pestle and hopped over the river.

Again the children heard her behind them and threw down the comb. This time, a forest appeared full of dark trees of matted roots and leaves. The witch tried this way, she tried that way, but she just couldn't get through. With a huff and a puff, she returned home.

The orphans rushed to their father, told him everything about their stepmother, and said to him, "Our dear father, why do you love us less than our brothers and sisters?"

The father was very angry. He sent the wicked stepmother away and dedicated the rest of his life to his own two children.

THE WOODEN EAGLE

In a certain kingdom, in a certain land, there lived a tsar. And this tsar had many servants. But these were not simply servants (such as any old tsar might have). No, this tsar collected craftsmen as others collect trinkets: carpenters, potters, and tailors. The tsar loved his clothing to be sewn better than all others, his dishes to be more cunningly painted, and the palace to be decorated with the most elaborate carvings.

The number of master craftsmen in the royal palace was ridiculous. In the mornings they all gathered for a special royal audience and awaited the king's command. Every day, he would give them a new task.

It so happened that a goldsmith and a carpenter bumped into one another in front of the royal palace. They bumped into one another and started arguing—which of them knows his craft better and whose work is more difficult.

The goldsmith said, "Your skill is not great, you sit over wood, and cut wooden things. But I, I make everything from pure gold—it's a pleasure to look at."

The carpenter replied, "There is no real skill in making an expensive thing out of gold, for gold itself is valuable. Make something from simple wood that will amaze everyone, and then I will believe that you are a master."

They argued, argued so much that they nearly came to blows. At that moment, the tsar entered. He overheard this conversation, grinned and then gave them an order:

"Both of you make me some sort of curiosity: one of gold, one of wood. I will look at them and decide which of you is the better master."

One shouldn't argue with tsars, for life is precious. The masters went from the palace, each to his own workshop, both deep in thought about how to surpass the other in skill.

The tsar gave them a week.

A week later, both artisans came to the palace, stood in line with the others, and waited for the tsar to arrive. Each held a bundle in his hands.

The tsar came out and said, "Well done, go on and show your craft," with a grin stretched out across his beard.

He ordered the tsaritsa and the young prince to be called into the chamber. "Let them take a look at your work."

The tsar and tsaritsa sat down on a bench, and the prince stood next to them. The goldsmith stepped forward and said, "Tsar-father, please order a large vat of water to be brought."

A large vat was brought and filled with water.

The master untied his bundle, took out a golden duck from it and put it into the water. The duck swam as if it were alive: turning its head, quacking, and cleaning its feathers with its beak.

The tsar opened his mouth in surprise, and the tsaritsa shouted, "Oh, but this is a live duck, not a golden one! He just covered a live duck with gold!"

The master was offended. "Of course, it is not alive! Order me to take it apart piece by piece and put it back together again."

He took the duck out of the tub, first unscrewed its wings,

then its head, and then took it all apart. Then he laid it out on the table, and screwed it together again.

Having wound it up he let it back into the water. And the duck swam, even better than before.

All the courtiers clapped their hands. "You are quite the craftsman! What a miracle you have created! I have not seen such a thing in all my years!"

The tsar turned to the carpenter. "Now show us your craft."

The carpenter bowed. "Your royal majesty, if you please, order a window be opened in this room."

A window was opened. The carpenter unfolded his bundle and took a wooden eagle out of it. The eagle was so well made that it was indistinguishable from a living one. And the carpenter said, "A golden duck only swims on the water, but my eagle rises up into the clouds."

The carpenter sat on the eagle and turned a clockwork mechanism. The eagle picked him up and instantly flew up into the air and out of the royal chamber. Everyone rushed to the windows, looking on with their mouths agape, as the carpenter flew above the royal court making circles in the air. He turned the screw to the left and the eagle flew downward, turned it to the right and the eagle ascended into the air. The tsar was so surprised and in such awe that his crown slid down to the back of his head. He looked out the window and couldn't tear himself away from what he was seeing. Everyone seemed to be frozen. No one had ever seen the like!

The carpenter circled through the air and flew back into the room. Setting the eagle aside, he approached the king. "Well, Tsar-father, are you pleased with my craft?"

"I am at a loss for words, I'm so pleased," the tsar answered. "How did you manage to do that? How did you attach this screw to him?"

As the carpenter began to explain to the king, the tsaritsa

gasped and screamed, "Where are you going? Where? Catch him, stop him!"

Everyone turned around and saw: while the tsar was speaking with the carpenter, the young prince jumped onto the eagle, turned the screw—and flew out of the window into the courtyard.

"Come back this instant! Where are you going? You will get yourself killed!" the tsar and tsaritsa shouted out to him.

But the prince waved his hand at them and flew over the silver fence that surrounded the palace. He turned the screw to the right, and the eagle rose up beyond the clouds and disappeared from sight.

The tsaritsa lay unconscious, and the tsar was very angry. But he had no one to direct his anger at, so he chose the poor carpenter.

"This thing," he said, "you purposely invented such a thing to kill our only son. Guards! Seize him and throw him into the dungeon. If the prince does not return in two weeks, hang the carpenter on the gallows."

The guards grabbed the carpenter and threw him into a dark dungeon.

All the while, the prince flew further and further on the wooden eagle.

The prince marveled. How spacious, empty, and free it was all around him. How the wind whistled in his ears, and his curls fluttered. How the clouds rushed under his feet—the prince himself was like a winged bird. Wherever he wanted, there he flew.

By evening, he flew to an unknown kingdom and descended to the edge of the city. Here he spotted a small hut.

The prince knocked on the door, and an old woman looked out.

"Let me in, granny, to spend the night. I'm a stranger here, I don't know anyone and have no one to stay with."

"Why not? Come in, there's plenty of room. I live alone."

The prince turned the eagle off, tied it into a bundle, and walked into the old woman's hut.

The old woman fed him dinner, and the prince asked, "What kind of city is this, who lives in it, what curiosities does it contain?"

The old lady responded, "We have but one miracle in the land, my son. The royal palace stands in the middle of the city, and near the palace there is a high tower. The tower is locked with thirty locks, and its gates are guarded by thirty watchmen. No one is allowed into that tower. And the king's daughter lives there. As soon as she was born, they locked her up in that tower with her nanny so that no one could see her. The tsar and tsaritsa are afraid that the princess will fall in love with someone and they will have to give her away in marriage. They do not want to part with her: she is their only child. So the girl lives in the tower, as if in a dungeon."

"And is it true? Is it true that the princess is that beautiful?" the prince asked.

"I don't know, son, I have never seen her myself, but people say that such beauty cannot be found in the whole world."

And just like that, the prince decided to get into the forbidden tower. He lay down to sleep, but all he could think about was the princess.

The next day, as soon as it got dark, he sat on his wooden eagle, soared into the clouds, and flew to the tower, to the side where the window was.

He flew up to the window and knocked on the glass.

The princess was surprised by the sight of such a handsome young man at her window.

"Who are you, kind youth?" she asked.

"Open the window, and I'll tell you everything, this very moment."

The girl opened the window, and the wooden eagle flew into the room. The prince got down from the eagle, greeted the princess, and told her who he was and how he got there.

They sat looking at one another—unable to take their eyes off each other.

The prince asked the princess to become his wife.

"Very well," said the princess, "but I'm afraid that my father and mother will not release me."

All the while, the evil nanny who kept watch over the princess had seen everything. She ran to the palace and reported that a youth had come and flown to the princess, and now this young man was hiding at the old woman's house.

The guards came running, grabbed the prince, and dragged him to the palace. There the tsar sat on the throne, red with anger and knocking on the floor with his club.

"How did you, some common robber, dare to violate my royal ban? Tomorrow I will order you to be executed!"

They took the prince to the dungeon and locked him up in his own cell with strong locks.

In the morning, all the people were driven to the square. It was announced that the impudent youth who entered the tower would be executed.

The executioner had come, and the gallows were set up, and the tsar himself and the tsaritsa came to watch the execution.

They took the prince to the square. He turned to the tsar and said, "Your Majesty, allow me to make one last request."

The tsar frowned, but it was impossible for him to refuse.

"Well, speak then."

"Order the messenger to run to the house, to the old woman where I lived, and to bring my bundle."

Unable to refuse, the tsar sent a messenger. The package was brought.

By then the prince was already up on the gallows and put on a ladder. The messenger gave him the package.

The prince unwrapped it, jumped on the wooden eagle— and that was that. He soared over the gallows, over the king, over the whole crowd.

The tsar gasped. "Catch him! Seize him! He will fly away!"

The prince directed the eagle to the tower, flew to the familiar window, picked up the princess and sat her on the eagle in front of him.

"Well," he said, "no one will be able to catch us now, we have nothing to fear."

And the eagle rushed them away to the kingdom of the prince. There the poor carpenter sat in the dungeon, his eyes on the sky, wondering—is the prince flying back? Tomorrow will be two weeks since the prince flew away, and the carpenter will hang on a rope if the king's son does not return.

And suddenly he sees—a wooden eagle flying across the sky, and on it is the prince, but not alone. He is with a beautiful girl!

The eagle descended in the middle of the royal court. The prince took his bride down from the eagle and took her to his father and mother. He told them where he had been for the past two weeks. In their great joy they forgave him the anxiety he had caused them, and the carpenter was released from the dungeon.

The tsar arranged a great feast. As for the wedding . . . it was celebrated for three months, not a day less!

Once upon a time, very long ago, there was a little Prince Ivan who, poor lamb, couldn't speak a word. Not so much as a "yes" or a "no," or a "please" or a "thank you." His father the tsar worried constantly. I'm sure you can understand—what good is an heir who can't speak? In fact, neither his father nor his mother could bear the sight of him. Sometimes, when things were especially bad, they said this terrible prayer: "If only we could have another child, whatever it is like, it couldn't possibly be worse than this silent child who cannot say a word." Not a good idea, as I'm sure you agree.

They took no care of the little Prince Ivan, and he spent all his time in the stables, listening to the tales of an old groom.

He was a wise man, was this old groom. He knew all kinds of stories, and perhaps that's why he had strange, unexpected wisdom about things. He could tell things were about to happen before they did. He anticipated changes in weather. And he did it all with a twinkle in his eye and gentle compassion for poor little Ivanushka.

One day, the groom was more than usually worried. "Ivanushka," he said, "I have terrible news for you, my boy.

This morning, you have a new sister, and a bad one at that. She has come because of your father's prayers and your mother's wishes. A witch she is, and she will grow like a stalk of wheat. In six weeks she'll be a grown witch, and with her iron teeth she will eat your father and eat your mother. She'll chew you up, too, if she gets the chance. There's nothing you can do for your parents. They've made their bed already. But if you are smart and quick and listen to me, you may escape your witch-baby sister. God knows I love you, my little dumb Ivanushka, and do not wish to think of your little body crushed by her iron teeth. So this is what you must do. You must go to your father and ask him for the best horse he has, and then gallop like the wind, and away to the end of the world."

Little Prince Ivan ran off and found his father. There was his father, and there was his mother, and a little baby girl was in his mother's arms, screaming like a little fury.

"Well, at least *she's* not dumb," said his father, very well pleased.

Then little Prince Ivan opened his mouth . . . and spoke! "Father," he said, "may I have the fastest horse in the stable?" Yes, indeed, those were the first words that had ever left his mouth.

"What!" said his father, "have you got a voice at last? Yes, take whatever horse you want. Now look, you have a little sister; a fine little girl she is, too. She has teeth already. It's a pity they are black, but time will put that right, and it's better to have black teeth than to be born dumb."

Little Prince Ivan shook in his little boots when he heard of his witch-sister's black teeth. He knew that they were iron. Thanking his father, he ran off to the stable. The old groom saddled the finest horse the tsar had. Such a horse you never saw. Black it was, and its saddle and bridle were trimmed with shining silver. And little Prince Ivan climbed up and sat on the great black horse, and waved his hand to the old groom, and galloped away, seeking the very end of the world.

"It's a big place, this world," thought little Prince Ivan. "I wonder when I shall come to the end of it."

On and on galloped little Prince Ivan on his great black warrior-horse. There were no houses anywhere to be seen. It was a long time since they had passed any people, and little Prince Ivan began to feel very lonely indeed. Perhaps he had truly come to the end of the world already?

Suddenly, he rode out of a dark forest into a clearing, where he saw two old, old women sitting under an oak tree.

They were bent double over their work, sewing and sewing, and now one and now the other broke a needle, and took a new one out of a box between them, and threaded the needle with thread from another box, and went on sewing and sewing. Their old noses nearly touched their knees as they bent over their work.

Little Prince Ivan pulled up the great black horse in a cloud of dust.

"Grandmothers," said he, "is this the end of the world? Let me stay here and live with you, and be safe from my baby sister, who is a witch and has iron teeth. Please let me stay with you. I'll be very little trouble and thread your needles for you when you break them."

"Prince Ivan, my dear," said one of the old women, "this is not the end of the world, and little good would it be to you to stay with us. For as soon as we have broken all our needles and used up all our thread, we shall die, and then where would you be? Your sister with the iron teeth would have you in a minute."

The little prince cried bitterly, for he was very little and all alone. He rode on further over the wide world, his black horse galloping and galloping, and throwing the dust from his thundering hooves.

He came into another forest of great oaks, the biggest oak trees he had ever seen. And in that forest was a dreadful noise —the crashing of trees falling, the breaking of branches, and the whistling of things hurled through the air. The prince rode on, and there before him was the huge giant Tree-twirler, pulling the great oaks out of the ground and flinging them aside like weeds.

"I should be safe with him," thought little Prince Ivan, "and this, surely, must be the end of the world."

He rode close up under the giant, and stopped the black horse, and shouted up into the air.

"Please, great giant," says he, "is this the end of the world? And may I live with you and be safe from my sister, who is a witch, and grows like a stalk of wheat, and has terrible black iron teeth?"

"Prince Ivan, my dear," says Tree-twirler, "this is not the end of the world, and little good would it be to you to stay with me. For as soon as I have pulled up all these trees, I shall die, and then where would you be? Your sister would have you in a minute. And already there are not many big trees left."

The giant set to work again, pulling up the great trees and twirling them as he cast them aside. The sky was full of flying trees.

Little Prince Ivan cried bitterly, for he was very little and was all alone. He rode on further over the wide world, the black horse galloping and galloping under the tall trees and throwing clods of earth from his thundering hooves.

He came out of the forest and into the steppe. In the distance, he saw the dim outline of tall mountains. Even from this distance, he heard a roaring and a crashing in those mountains as if the earth were falling to pieces. One after another whole mountains were lifted up into the sky and flung down to earth, so that they broke and scattered into dust. Still, the big black horse galloped through the mountains, and little Prince Ivan sat bravely on his back. And there, close before him, was the huge giant Mountain-tosser, picking up the mountains like pebbles and hurling them to little pieces and dust upon the ground.

"This must be the end of the world," thought the little prince; "and at any rate I should be safe with him."

"Please, great giant," says he, "is this the end of the world? And may I live with you and be safe from my sister, who is a witch, and has iron teeth, and grows like a stalk of wheat?"

"Prince Ivan, my dear," says Mountain-tosser, resting for a moment and dusting the rocks off his great hands, "this is not the end of the world, and little good would it be to you to stay with me. For as soon as I have picked up all these mountains and thrown them down again, I shall die, and then where would you be? Your sister would have you in a minute. And there are not very many mountains left."

And the giant set to work again, lifting up the great mountains and hurling them away. The sky was full of flying mountains.

Little Prince Ivan wept bitterly, for he was very little and was all alone. He rode on further over the wide world, the black horse galloping and galloping along the mountain paths, and throwing the stones from his thundering hooves.

At last he came to the end of the world, and there, hanging in the sky above him, was the castle of the little sister of the sun.

"I should be safe up there," thought little Prince Ivan, and just then the sun's little sister opened the window and beckoned to him.

Prince Ivan patted the big black horse and whispered to it, and it leapt up high into the air and through the window, into the very courtyard of the castle.

"Stay here and play with me," said the little sister of the sun; and Prince Ivan tumbled off the big black horse into her arms and laughed because he was so happy.

Merry and pretty was the sun's little sister, and she was very kind to little Prince Ivan. They played games together, and when she was tired she let him do whatever he liked and run about her castle. This way and that he ran about the battlements of rosy cloud, hanging in the sky over the end of the world.

But one day he climbed up and up to the topmost turret of the castle. From there he could see the whole world. And far, far away, beyond the mountains, beyond the forests, beyond the steppes, he saw his father's palace where he had been born. The roof of the palace was gone, and the walls were broken and crumbling. And little Prince Ivan came slowly down from the turret, and his eyes were red with weeping.

"My dear," said the sun's little sister, "why are your eyes so red?"

"It was very windy up there," said little Prince Ivan.

And the sun's little sister put her head out of the window of the castle of cloud and whispered to the winds not to blow so hard.

But next day little Prince Ivan went up again to that topmost turret, and looked far away over the wide world to the ruined palace. "She has eaten them all with her iron teeth," he said to himself. And his eyes were red when he came down.

"My dear," says the sun's little sister, "your eyes are red again."

"It is only the wind," says little Prince Ivan.

And the sun's little sister put her head out of the window and scolded the wind.

But the third day again little Prince Ivan climbed up the stairs of cloud to that topmost turret, and looked far away to the broken palace where his father and mother had lived. And he came down from the turret with the tears running down his face.

"Why, you are crying again, my dear!" says the sun's little sister. "Tell me what is the matter."

So little Prince Ivan told the little sister of the sun how his sister was a witch, and how he wept to think of his father and mother, and how he had seen the ruins of his father's palace far away, and how he could not stay with her happily until he knew how it was with his parents.

"Perhaps it is not yet too late to save them from her iron teeth, though the old groom said that she would certainly eat them. But let me ride back on my big black horse."

"Do not leave me, my dear," said the sun's little sister. "I am lonely here by myself."

"I will ride back on my big black horse, and then I will come to you again."

"What must be, must be," said the sun's little sister, sighing. "She is more likely to eat you than you are to save them. You shall go. But take these gifts with you first: a magic comb, a magic brush, and two apples of youth. These apples will make young once more even the oldest things on earth."

Then she kissed little Prince Ivan, he climbed up on his big black horse, and he leapt out of the window of the castle down on the end of the world, and galloped off on his way back over the wide world.

He came to Mountain-tosser, the giant. There was only one mountain left, and the giant was just picking it up. Sadly he was picking it up, for he knew that when he had thrown it away his work would be done and he would have to die.

"Well, little Prince Ivan," said Mountain-tosser, "this is the end." He heaved up the final mountain. But before he could toss it away the little Prince threw his magic brush on the plain, and the brush swelled and burst, and suddenly there was range upon range of high mountains, touching the sky itself.

"Why," says Mountain-tosser, "I have enough mountains now to last me for another thousand years. Thank you kindly, Ivanushka."

And he set to work again, heaving up mountains and tossing them down, while little Prince Ivan galloped on across the wide world.

He came to Tree-twirler, the giant. There were only two of the great oaks left, and the giant had one in each hand.

"Ah me, little Prince Ivan," said Tree-twirler, "my life is come to its end; for I have only to pluck up these two trees and throw them down, and then I shall die."

"Pluck them up," says little Prince Ivan. "Here are plenty more for you." And he threw down his comb. There was a noise of spreading branches, of swishing leaves, of opening buds, all together, and there before them was a forest of great oaks stretching farther than the giant could see, tall though he was.

"Why," says Tree-twirler, "here are enough trees to last me for another thousand years. Thank you kindly, Ivanushka."

He set to work again, pulling up the big trees, laughing joyfully and hurling them over his head, while little Prince Ivan galloped on across the wide world.

He came to the two old women.

"There is only one needle left!" said the first.

"There is only one bit of thread in the box!" sobbed the second.

"And then we shall die!" they said both together, mumbling with their old mouths.

"Here, eat these apples," said little Prince Ivan, and he gave them the two apples of youth.

The two old women took the apples in their old shaking fingers and ate them, bent double, mumbling with their old lips. No sooner had they finished their last mouthfuls than they sat up straight, smiled with sweet red lips, and looked at the little prince with shining eyes. They had become young girls again, and their gray hair was black as a raven's wing.

"Thank you kindly, Ivanushka," said the two young girls. "You must take with you the handkerchief we have been sewing all these years. Throw it to the ground, and it will turn into a lake of water. Perhaps someday it will be useful to you."

"Thank you," said the little prince, and off he galloped, on and on over the wide world.

He came at last to his father's palace. The roof was gone,

and there were holes in the walls. He left his horse at the edge of the garden, and crept up to the ruined palace and peeped through a hole. Inside, in the great hall, was sitting a huge baby girl, filling the whole hall. There was no longer any room for her to move. She had knocked off the roof with a shake of her head. And there she sat in the ruined hall, sucking her thumb.

Even while Prince Ivan was watching through the hole, he heard her mutter to herself, "Eaten the father, eaten the mother, and now to eat the little brother."

And she began shrinking, getting smaller and smaller every minute.

Little Prince Ivan had only just time to get away from the hole in the wall when a pretty little baby girl came running out of the ruined palace.

"You must be my little brother Ivan," she called out to him, and came up to him smiling. But as she smiled the little Prince saw that her teeth were black; and as she shut her mouth he heard them clink together like pokers.

"Come in," said she, and she took little Prince Ivan with her to a room in the palace, all broken down and cobwebbed. There was an old harp lying in the dust on the floor.

"Well, little brother," said the witch baby, "you play on the *gusli* and amuse yourself while I get supper ready. But don't stop playing, or I shall feel lonely." And she ran off and left him.

Little Prince Ivan sat down and played sad music on the old harp. You would not play dance music if you thought you were going to be eaten by a witch.

But while he was playing, a little gray mouse came out of a crack in the floor.

"Ivan, Ivan," said the little gray mouse, "run while you may. Your father and mother were eaten long ago, and well they deserved it. But be quick, or she will eat you too. Your pretty little sister is filing an edge to her iron witch-teeth!"

Little Prince Ivan thanked the mouse, ran out from the ruined palace, and climbed up on the back of his big black horse, with its saddle and bridle trimmed with silver. Away he galloped over the wide world. The witch baby stopped her work and listened. She heard the music of the gusli, so she made sure he was still there. She went on sharpening her teeth with a file, growing bigger and bigger every minute. And all the time the music of the gusli sounded mournfully among the ruins.

As soon as her teeth were sharp enough she rushed off to eat little Prince Ivan. She tore aside the walls of the room. There was nobody there—only a little gray mouse running and jumping this way and that on the strings of the gusli.

When it saw the witch baby, the little mouse ran across the floor and into the crack and away. How the witch baby gnashed her teeth! Poker and tongs, poker and tongs—what a noise they made! She swelled up, bigger and bigger, till she was a baby as tall as the palace. And then she jumped up so that the palace fell to pieces about her. Then off she ran after little Prince Ivan.

Little Prince Ivan, on the big black horse, heard a noise behind him. He looked back, and there was the huge witch, towering over the trees. She was dressed like a little baby, and her eyes flashed and her teeth clanged as she shut her mouth. She was running with long strides, faster even than the black horse could gallop—and he was the best horse in all the world.

Little Prince Ivan threw down the handkerchief that had been sewn by the two old women who had eaten the apples of youth. It turned into a deep, broad lake, so that the witch baby had to swim—and swimming is slower than running. It took her a long time to get across, and all that time Prince Ivan was galloping on, never stopping for a moment.

But the witch baby crossed the lake and came thundering after him. Close behind she was, and would have caught him; but the giant Tree-twirler saw the little prince galloping on the big black horse and the witch baby tearing after him. He pulled up the great oaks in armfuls and threw them down just in front of the witch baby. He made a huge pile of the big trees, and the witch baby had to stop and gnaw her way through them with her iron teeth.

It took her a long time to gnaw through the trees, and the black horse galloped and galloped ahead. But soon Prince Ivan heard a noise behind him. He looked back, and there was the witch baby, thirty feet high, racing after him, clanging with her teeth. Close behind she was, and the little prince sat firm on the big black horse, and galloped and galloped. But she would have caught him if the giant Mountain-tosser had not seen the little prince on the big black horse and the great witch baby running after him. The giant tore up the biggest mountain in the world and flung it down in front of her, and another on the top of that. She had to bite her way through them, while the little Prince galloped and galloped.

At last little Prince Ivan saw the castle of the little sister of the sun, hanging over the end of the world and gleaming in the sky. He shouted with hope, and the black horse shook his head proudly and galloped on. The witch baby thundered after him. Nearer she came and nearer.

"Ah, little Ivan," screamed the witch baby, "you won't get away this time!"

The little sister of the sun was looking from a window of the castle in the sky, and she saw the witch baby stretching out to grab little Prince Ivan. She flung the window open, and just in time the big black horse leapt up, through the window and into the courtyard, with little Prince Ivan safe on its back.

How the witch baby gnashed her iron teeth!

"Give him up!" she screamed.

"I will not," said the sun's little sister.

"Now see here!" said the witch baby, and she makes herself smaller and smaller and smaller, till she was just like a real little girl. "Let us be weighed in the great scales, and if I am heavier than Prince Ivan, I can take him; and if he is heavier than I am, I'll say no more about it."

The sun's little sister laughed at the witch baby and teased her, but still she hung the great scales out of the cloud castle so that they swung above the end of the world.

Little Prince Ivan got into one scale, and down it went.

"Now," says the witch baby, "we shall see."

And she made herself bigger and bigger and bigger, till she was as big as she had been when she sat and sucked her thumb in the hall of the ruined palace. "I am the heavier," she shouted, and gnashed her iron teeth. Then she jumped into the other scale.

She was so heavy that the scale with the little prince in it shot up into the air. It shot up so fast that little Prince Ivan flew up into the sky, up and up and up, and came down on the topmost turret of the cloud castle of the little sister of the sun.

The sun's little sister laughed, and closed the window, and went up to the turret to meet the little prince. But the witch baby turned back the way she had come and went off, gnashing her iron teeth until they broke. And ever since then, little Prince Ivan and the little sister of the sun play together in the castle of cloud that hangs over the end of the world.

Inspired by Arthur Ransome's telling
of the classic Russian fairy tale

THE TALE OF SADKO

In old Novgorod-town, there lived a fine young man named Sadko. He lived all alone, no hearth or home to his name. Nothing but his gusli—the finest harp in all Novgorod—and a talent that gave him a name. He was known by everyone as the best harpist in all the North.

His name rolled along the tongues of all the great in old Novgorod. The boyars called him to play in their halls of painted gold, the merchants in their houses built of white marble. Every feast, every wedding—they all had to have Sadko for their joy and their dancing and their merriment.

His hands moved like lightning, his voice was pure as the water of Ilmen-Lake outside the city. No one could get enough of that sound. That was all he did, and it was all the money he made. Going from dinner to feast to dinner to feast. And he loved every minute of it.

But merchants are famously fickle, as you all know, I'm sure. And so there came a time when a day passed without a single invitation to play at a feast. A second such day came, then a third! Can you imagine!

Sadko was wounded to the depths of his heart. Naturally, his stomach growled a bit as well, but it was the insult that rankled. He shook his fist at the high-gabled houses of merchants and nobles in old Novgorod-town, and he took his gusli and walked through the gates of the city. There he sought his favorite place to sit and play—a perfect brooding-rock by Lake Ilmen. There he made himself comfortable and strummed his gusli at the rising sun. He played to his heart's content the whole day through, until the sun started to come back down, and the waters of the lake seemed to burble at the sun's descent.

Then, Sadko saw that there was no *seeming* about it. The waters were spinning in a most unhealthy way. Suddenly, a wave rose up like a hill, the water mixed up with sand on the beach, and the master of Ilmen Lake himself appeared, all wet and glorious. The harpist froze in his tracks. But the master of the lake said:

"Thank you, dear Sadko of Novgorod! Today I held a feast in my watery halls, and you gave much joy and pleasure to my guests. I want to reward you for your pains!

"Now listen carefully. Tomorrow, you will be called by a first among merchants to play at a feast for the greatest of Novgorod's merchants. They will eat, they will drink, and they will begin to do what they love to do the most. They will start boasting. One will boast of his countless gold coins, another will speak of his priceless foreign treasures, a third will boast of his horses or his house. Perhaps there will be a wise one or two who will boast in his parentage, or a fool who will boast of his young wife.

"Then, the merchants will ask you what you can boast of, Sadko the poor. And I will teach you an answer that will make you richer than them all!"

And that is exactly what the master of Lake Ilmen did.

As he promised, the very next day, Sadko was called to play at a great feast of assembled merchants, the best in the city.

The tables were breaking under the weight of food and drink. And the merchants tucked in with a vengeance. It did not take long for their liquid joy to start pouring out in their foolish boasting. One boasted of his countless gold coins, another spoke of his priceless foreign treasures. A third wisely boasted of his parents, and, yes indeed, there was one fool there who boasted of his young wife.

And then, having boasted their fill, they turned to Sadko the harpist.

"And what of you, young man? What can you boast of?"

Sadko took a deep breath, and answered as the master of Ilmen instructed him: "O you wise, wealthy merchants! What can I possibly boast of before you great ones? You yourselves know that I have not a penny to my name, nor do I have a storefront along main street in old Novgorod town. And yet, there is one thing I can boast of. I alone know of a wondrous thing, a true miracle of miracles.

"There is—in our own Lake Ilmen, of all -places—a fish with a golden feather! And no one has seen this fish, not seen it or caught it even. But whoever will catch this fish with the golden feather and make fish soup out of it will become young again. That is all I can boast of in this wide world of ours!"

Immediately, the hall erupted with voices. "You are a fool, Sadko, to boast of such things. No one from the beginning of time has ever heard of such a thing as a fish with a golden feather, or that if you make soup of such a fish, an old man will become young again!"

Six of the greatest merchants of Novgorod were especially querulous. "There is no such fish, Sadko. We will make a great wager with you. All of our storefronts and all our riches we wager, and you need offer only one thing—the fish with the golden feather. But if you fail in your wager, on your head be it!"

"I agree to your wager," cried Sadko the harpist. "And my own head I wager in return."

They spat in their palms and shook on it, all of them.

Immediately, the merchants had their men weave a net out

of silk and Sadko took it. He threw it into the waters of Ilmen-Lake, and he caught a fish with a golden feather! A second time he tossed the net in, and he pulled out another such fish! And a third time he cast his net, and a third time he caught a fish with a golden feather.

The master of Ilmen-Lake had kept his word and rewarded Sadko generously. The orphan-harpist won for himself the riches of the greatest merchants of the city. Nor did he waste his newfound good fortune. He traded with the best of them and showed himself a shrewd and wise merchant, no slouch in money as he was no slouch in music. Soon he was the richest man in that richest of all old Russian cities. He built himself a house of white marble, decorated his living room with carved mahogany. Everywhere silver, gold, and crystal sparkled in the light of hundreds of candles. No one had ever seen such a house, nor even imagined such a place.

Soon afterward young Sadko married and brought his young wife into his home. To celebrate this great event, he called all the greatest of Novgorod to a feast the likes of which they had never seen. Everyone found a place at this feast of feasts, even the common men of old Novgorod. The food and drink threatened to break the tables in half, and the joy of those feasting rose with every passing hour.

Sadko walked among the many tables and said to his guests, "My dear guests, you nobles with your tall hats and you merchants with your endless wealth, and you, commoners of our great city. All of you have eaten of my food, have drunk of my cellars, and now you waste your time in idle boasting. Some of you boast in truth, others lie to my face. It seems that it is time for me to speak as well. But what shall I, Sadko, boast of? I have no peer in wealth. I have enough gold that I could buy every single item in every single store in Novgorod, and still I would have money left over. But Novgorod itself would be empty!"

Such proud words seemed offensive to everyone—noble,

merchant, and commoner alike. And the noise of their complaining rose high above his head.

"There never was a time, and there never shall be, when a single man can buy out all the goods of Novgorod the great, our glorious city! And so we will raise a great wager against you, Sadko, you great man of our great city. Forty thousand we will wager! No matter how rich a single man may be, he is nothing more than a reed in the wind compared to the greatest of all cities and its eminent people!"

But Sadko would not budge from his boast, and he took their wager. And that was the end of that strangest of feasts.

The next morning, Sadko rose before the sun, washed, and got dressed in his best. He woke his faithful servants, filled their bags with uncounted piles of gold, and sent them out to the markets of great Novgorod to buy out all the goods in that great city. From morning to evening, Sadko himself and every one of his followers bought out every single item in every single merchant stall in that greatest of cities. By evening, there was not a single item left in the city!

But then, the next day came, and the merchants returned from their long journeys with carts full of items from all over Rus and beyond.

So Sadko got up the next morning and bought them all out again!

The third morning, Sadko got up early with his servants to see if there were anything more in the city for him to purchase. And lo and behold! The stores were full, and the merchants' stalls were overflowing yet again! And Sadko overheard the merchants whispering of caravans still coming from Moscow itself, from Tver, and from many other cities, not to mention all the ships coming from lands beyond the Rus.

And Sadko grew thoughtful.

"It seems I can't defeat great Novgorod or buy out all the cities of the Rus from the face of the earth. It seems that no matter how rich I am, Novgorod the great is still the richer.

Better for me to lose forty thousand than everything else. I now see and admit, there is no one man who can withstand the glory of a city and its eminent men."

And Sadko admitted defeat and paid the forty thousand. Still, he had enough left over to build forty ships. He put all he had onto those forty ships and left for distant, exotic lands to trade. In those distant lands, he sold the goods of Novgorod at a great profit to himself.

But on the way home, disaster finally struck this luckiest of Novgorod's men. All forty ships, in the middle of the Caspian Sea with no land in sight, suddenly stood still as though they had landed on a hidden island. The wind tore at their sails and pulled at their masts, the waves beat at the sides of the ships, but the forty ships sat there, as though in peaceful anchorage.

And Sadko said to his faithful men, "It seems that the tsar of the sea demands a tax. Take a barrel of gold and throw it overboard!"

They did so, but still the ships did not budge.

"The tsar of the sea doesn't accept our offering, it seems. Perhaps the payment he demands is a human soul."

And he commanded that lots be drawn. Everyone else pulled a linden branch, while Sadko pulled an oak branch. They threw theirs overboard. The linden branches—every single one of them—floated as if they were ducks. And the single oaken branch sank to the bottom of the sea.

"Of course," said Sadko, "linden is lighter than oak. Mine needs to be of linden as well."

So he pulled for himself a linden branch and threw it overboard. Still, it was the only one to sink like a stone to the depths.

"What can we do, brothers? It seems the tsar of the sea has no interest in anyone's head but my own!"

Then he took a piece of paper and a quill, and he wrote down his will. He left generous gifts to all his people, and he didn't forget to leave money to the monastery, asking for prayers for the dead. He left much of his wealth to the poor, the widows, the orphaned, and especially his young wife. After this, he said, "Put down a firm oaken board, my friends. It would be frightful to go down to the waters on my own."

They did so. Then Sadko said goodbye to his people and grabbed his trusty gusli with him. "I'll play on the board for the final time before death takes me!"

And so saying, Sadko was lowered to the oaken board, and immediately all forty ships launched forward, their silken sails filling with wind, and on they followed the way back home.

There sat Sadko on an oaken board, playing his gusli mournfully, remembering all his previous days. The waves gently swayed him back and forth, and he didn't even notice that he fell deeply asleep, his gusli still in his hands.

How long did he sleep? Who knows? But when he finally awoke, he was on the floor of the ocean-sea, at the gates of a marvelous palace. From that palace a servant ran out and led Sadko in. There, in a wide, expansive throne room, sat the tsar of the sea himself. His hoary head was adorned with gold. And the tsar of the sea spoke aloud:

"Well met, dear guest, so long-awaited! Much have I heard of your talents from my nephew, the master of Ilmen-Lake. And I wanted to hear you for myself. That is why I stopped your ships and chose your lot from all others."

Then he called his slave. "Prepare a bathhouse for our guest! Surely he is exhausted from his journey. Let him wash and rest a while. Then, we will feast! Soon the guests will start assembling."

That evening, the tsar of the sea hosted a feast of feasts. Various lords and lordlings came from all bodies of water all over the world. There was the master of Ilmen-Lake as well. The tables at that feast were breaking from the weight of the food and the drink. Eat and drink to your heart's content! And the guests did exactly that.

Then the host, the tsar of the sea, said, "Well, Sadko,

would you give us the joy of your playing? Nothing somber now, something to make the feet dance of their own accord!"

And that's exactly what Sadko did. No guest was able to remain at table. They all jumped out from their seats and entered the dance, and they danced so feverishly that the Caspian Sea itself seemed to boil, so harsh was the storm on the surface. That day, many ships capsized, and many men fell to the depths!

The harpist plays, and the lords of the sea dance and dance, crying out, "Play on, play on!"

Then, suddenly, Sadko heard the whisper of his old friend, the master of Ilmen-Lake, at his left ear.

"This is not a good thing that my uncle has started. You have no idea what sort of storm all this dancing has caused up in the overworld. Many people have perished today from the dancing of the tsar of the sea. You must stop, the dancing must stop!"

"How can I stop? Here at the bottom of the sea, my will is not my own. Until your uncle, the tsar of the sea, commands it, I am not able to stop."

"Here's what you do. Pretend to accidentally break a string or two on that harp of yours. Say that you have no spares. As soon as you cease, all the guests will come back to themselves and the feast will end. But the tsar of the sea will seek to keep you here forever. To do this, he will try to seduce you with the promise of a watery bride. But you must not agree. No matter how beautiful these daughters of his seem—and they are all the most beautiful women in the world! Three hundred beauties will present themselves to you, then another three hundred—all of them of beauty that no pen can describe, no story can tell. But you stand there and be silent. Another three hundred will pass before you, even more beautiful than those before. But you let them all pass, choose the final one, and say, 'That is the one, dear Chernavushka, I want to marry her!' She is my own dear sister, and she will save you from this place."

Thus spoke the master of Ilmen-Lake, and disappeared into the crowd.

Sadko broke a string, as though by accident, and said to the tsar of the sea, "I have no spares with me, O king of the lower lands!"

"Ah, Sadko, where would I find such a thing in my palace? Tomorrow I will send out couriers to find what you need. But for today, we have feasted enough."

The next day, the tsar of the sea called Sadko to himself. "You must remain here, Sadko, and be my faithful harpist. All the watery lords have fallen in love with your playing. As a reward, I will give you any beautiful princess of the sea, and you will live in my tsardom with much more glory than in dear old Novgorod. Choose a bride!"

The tsar of the sea clapped his hands twice, and suddenly a line of beautiful maidens passed by Sadko, each more beautiful than the one before. Three hundred passed him by. After them, another three hundred passed, all so beautiful that no pen could describe them, no tale could tell of them. But Sadko stood there, silent. After these, another three hundred walked by, even more beautiful. Sadko looked with pleasure, but remained silent. Finally, he saw the final girl, and he pointed at her.

"I have chosen a bride for myself. I wish to marry this beautiful maiden!"

"A fine choice, Sadko the harpist! You have chosen a good bride, for she is my own niece! Chernava the river. Now you and I will be family."

And they celebrated a great wedding feast that very night. When the feasting ended, the newly married couple went to their bridal chamber. No sooner did the doors close than Chernava said to Sadko, "Go to sleep, Sadko, and worry for nothing. As my own brother commanded me, so shall everything be."

And a wave of deep slumber overwhelmed Sadko.

When he woke up in the morning, he simply couldn't believe his eyes: there he was, sitting on the banks of the Chernava River at the exact place where it empties into the Volkhov River by Novgorod. And right on Volkhov itself, forty ships were sailing, filled with his people and his goods.

They saw Sadko on the banks and wondered aloud: "We thought that we left Sadko in the depths of the ocean-sea, but here he is to meet us at the gates of our dear Novgorod! Miracles follow this man, brothers, like a shadow!"

They sent out a coracle for Sadko, and he joined them aboard. Soon the ships approached the harbor of the great city itself. All the foreign goods, all the golden coins were unloaded and carried into the cellars of Sadko the merchant.

And as he approached, his own dear beautiful wife ran out to meet him, throwing herself into his embrace, kissing him on his forehead and his eyes.

"O my dear husband, I had a dream tonight that you would return from your distant journeys. You must tell me all about them."

Sadko smiled to himself. Perhaps he would not tell her *all* that had happened.

They ate and they drank and they rested after their travels. And Sadko the merchant lived with his beautiful wife in peace and harmony and joy to the end of his days. And they were, I hear, quite long indeed.

THE CHESTNUT ROAN

In a certain kingdom, in a certain land, there lived a peasant who had three sons. The first two were fine fellows: they were good looking, strong, and always knew what to do in the field. They were the pride and joy of their father.

And then there was the third son, Ivan. He was a bit of an idiot. He liked to lie on the ledge of the big stove in the central room of the hut. He would lie there all day and do nothing.

One year, the peasant's crop of wheat yielded more than ever before. The wheat was tall, thick, and so juicy you could almost eat it raw. The peasant was very excited for the day he would sell it at the market and become rich.

But there was a problem. At night, someone began to come and trample the wheat fields. The strangest part was that the intruder didn't steal the wheat; he just trampled it to bits in what could only be described as terrible, ruinous carnage.

The father turned to his eldest son, who was the strongest and best looking, and said, "My son, go into my fields, capture this intruder, and bring him to me so that I may punish him."

So the eldest son took a little food and went out into the

fields. It was cold, however, so he soon found his way into the warm granary, climbed into the hayloft, and slept the soundest sleep of his life.

In the morning, he came to his father and said, "Father, I stayed awake all night and saw nothing."

Yet half the field was trampled!

So the father turned to his second son and said, "Now it is in your hands, my dear boy. Find this thief and bring him to me. He must be punished."

The second son went out, saw that there was a path leading directly to the granary, and thought how nice it would be to have a proper sleep. So he went and slept the whole night through.

In the morning, he came to his father and said, "Father, I stayed awake all night and saw nothing."

Yet again, the field was badly trampled. Finally, the father turned to his third son, who was lying on the shelf of the stove with a bit of drool coming out of the corner of his mouth.

He said, "Ivanushka, I have no one else. Please, do me a favor: get off your butt and go find that thief."

Ivanushka got up, stretched, scratched the back of his head, and said, "If you insist."

He took a large and delicious pie with him into the fields and found the most uncomfortable rock to sit on. Whenever his eyelids began to droop, he would grab a large bite of pie and stuff it into his mouth. The pie was so thick that chewing it was hard work.

So Ivanushka stayed awake, and in the middle of the night, the field became so bright that it looked as if it was the middle of the day! In the middle of the light was an enormous horse with a dappled coat of silver and gold. Its mane was like a storm. From its ears came steam, and from its nostrils came fire. This horse jumped and stamped around in the field with the pure joy of existence.

Ivanushka crept up behind it, threw a rope around its

neck, and held on for dear life. The huge horse jumped up and down, up and down, and almost flew into the air so that Ivanushka lost hold of the rope. But immediately he grabbed the horse's tail, holding on desperately as the horse thrashed.

At last the horse gave up and said, "Ivanushka, you have caught me. Only let me go, and I will give you whatever you desire."

Ivanushka scratched his very beardless chin and said, "I'll let you go, but you must promise never to trample our field again. And if I ever need you, how will I find you?"

The horse replied, "It's simple: go out into a field and scream like a warrior. Say, 'Chestnut Roan, wise and ancient steed, stand before my face like the forest before grass!' and I will appear to you."

Ivanushka thanked the horse, and the horse flew away. Then Ivanushka went home, and his father asked him what had happened.

He replied, "The culprit was a horse. I stopped him and made him promise never to do it again."

The brothers burst out laughing and cried, "What an idiot!"

And yet, from that time on, the wheat was never trampled again.

Time passed, and one day, an official came from the king.

He declared, "The king has announced a great event. His daughter the princess is to be wed, and not just to anyone, not even just to a prince! She is to be wed to anyone who is brave enough to catch her. She is sitting in the top of a tall, wide tower. If someone can jump with his horse all the way to the top of the tower and take off the ring from her finger, he shall have her as his bride."

The two brothers thought they might as well go and see what this was all about.

Ivanushka begged, "Brothers, will you give me a horse that

I may accompany you? Any old mule will do! I just want to come and see."

But the brothers spat at him and said, "Ivanushka, this is a place for real men. You stay here and don't bother us."

So they went. Ivanushka lay on the top of the stove and proceeded to be idle. But something nagged at him.

He sat up, turned to his sisters-in-law, and said, "Sisters-in-law, I am hungry. I want to go gather mushrooms. Will you give me a basket?"

Now these sisters-in-law did not think much more highly of Ivanushka than did his brothers, but they thought he could do no harm with a basket. So they gave him one, and Ivanushka went out until he found a field.

There he called, "Chestnut Roan, wise and ancient steed, stand before my face like the forest before grass!"

Suddenly, the horse appeared!

"How can I serve you, Ivanushka?"

"I want to see the princess, and I want to see her now."

The horse replied, "If you want to see her, climb into my right ear and out my left ear."

Ivanushka did so, and as he came out, what a fine looking prince he became! He had transformed into such a gorgeous young man that you can hardly describe it in words—you can only imagine it in tales. Ivanushka sat on the horse, and he rode like the wind to where the princess sat in her high tower.

Many people were gathered all around the tower, all pointing at the princess quite rudely. Yet none of them tried to jump to her for fear of breaking their necks. Ivanushka took one look at the tower and slapped the horse as hard as he could. The horse neighed and flew up so high that he was only three logs under the princess's window.

The crowd cried, "Stop him! Stop him!"

But Ivanushka turned around and rushed off, making sure to ride right by his brothers and smack them with his whip.

Ivanuhska returned to the field, thanked the horse,

grabbed several poisonous red-capped mushrooms, and returned to his sisters-in-law, saying, "Look, I brought us dinner!"

They looked contemptuously at him and said, "You can eat that. We're not touching it."

So Ivanushka lay back down on his ledge and waited.

When the brothers returned, they said, "There was an incredible young prince whose horse jumped so high he got very close to the princess!"

Ivanushka said, "Brothers, wasn't that me?"

They said, "Shut up, idiot! Of course it wasn't you—you weren't there!"

The next day, the same thing happened. Ivanushka begged to go with his brothers, but they refused. So Ivanushka went to gather mushrooms, called the steed, crawled into its right ear and out its left, and turned into a prince. They rode like the wind. This time, they jumped so high that they were only two logs away from the princess's window.

Everyone yelled, "Stop him! Stop him! Stop that beautiful young man!"

But Ivanushka rode off, making sure to ride right by his brothers and smack them with his whip. He went back to the field, grabbed a bunch of red-capped mushrooms, and brought them to his sisters-in-law, who again refused to eat them. Ivanushka went right back to his ledge, giggling a bit more than usual.

The brothers returned and said, "The incredible young man was there again, and no one could stop him! Who is he?"

Ivanushka said, "Brothers, wasn't that me?"

They said, "Shut up, idiot! Of course it wasn't you—you weren't there!"

On the third day, Ivanushka again crawled into the right ear of the horse and out its left ear. This time, he took the whip and slapped the horse. The horse flew, fire coming from its nostrils, and jumped right up to the window. The horse hung there in front of the window like a cloud. Ivanushka took the ring from off the princess's finger, and he even stole a kiss.

"Stop him! Stop him!" the crowd cried again. "He got the ring!"

But the horse was so fast that none could catch Ivanushka, who of course rode right by his brothers and smacked them with his whip.

That evening, when everyone was sitting around the hearth having private conversations, Ivnaushka couldn't help himself: for just a moment, he uncovered the ring. Suddenly, the entire hut was flooded with light, and Ivanushka had to hide the ring again quickly.

His brothers said, "Why are you playing with fire, you idiot? We're all going to burn!"

Ivanushka said nothing. A few days later, there was another summons from the king. The king said that everybody—yes, everybody—was invited to a wedding feast. It was a wedding without a groom, but never mind that! Everybody must be there, and if anyone failed to show up, his head would be cut off his shoulders.

This time the brothers had no choice. They had to take Ivanushka. So he went, covered in rags, unwashed, drool hanging from his chin. He was a sight to behold! He sat at the absolute last possible seat that he could in the king's palace.

Everyone had a wonderful time. The brothers had never tasted such delicious food, and the sisters-in-law went wild exclaiming over the quality of the soup!

Then the princess began to walk among the tables, giving everybody a drink from a special urn of wine. She even approached Ivanushka. Now Ivanushka had the ring wrapped up in one of the ugliest, dirtiest rags he could find.

The princess came to him and said, "Young man, what is it that you have under that rag? I would like to see it. Please uncover it."

So he did. The entire hall filled with an unearthly light.

The princess looked at him, took him by the hand, and dragged him to the king.

She said, "This is my husband!"

The king looked at Ivanushka and his eyes grew wide, but what was he to do? He was the one who had made the rules! So the servants took Ivanushka, washed him, and dressed him in new clothes. Suddenly, the beautiful young man who had arrived on the horse and kissed the princess was standing before them! No one had been able to see him because he had been so ugly, dirty, and smelly. But now his true self was revealed.

So the idiot married the princess. And I was there at the wedding feast. I drank a lot of mead. Unfortunately, a lot of it went down my mustache rather than into my mouth, but it was still quite lovely.

VASILISSA THE WISE AND THE KING OF UNDERLAND

In a certain kingdom, in a certain land, there lived a king and a queen. They lived together for many long years until the king grew restless. One fine day, he got up and left. He went on a long journey throughout all the kingdoms, as far as the eye could see.

While he was gone, his wife gave birth to a beautiful baby boy, and the king had no idea. He continued to journey for years. And after such a long, tiring journey, you can probably imagine just how thirsty he had become. He simply had to have water!

Suddenly, as though he had conjured it up from his imagination, there stretched before him a perfect, pristine lake. There was hardly a ripple on it. He could see all the way to the bottom.

The king came up to it, lay on his stomach, pulled his beard back, and drank the longest, most delicious drink of water he had ever tasted. But his joy was short-lived. Someone was tugging on his beard.

"Let go, let go!" he cried.

Looking down, he saw a king, just as bearded as he was, but coming up from the lake below him.

The king in the water said, "How dare you drink of my water without my permission!"

The king on land realized his mistake and said, "Please, let go of my beard! I will do anything you ask!"

The king in the water said, "Give me that which you do not know about at home."

The king thought to himself, *I don't even know what he means by that, but I'm sure I know all I have at home. It's probably nothing.*

As soon as the king agreed to this request, the beard was released, and the water king disappeared. The king on land, however, began to grow nervous. Something tickled the back of his mind, some dark doubt. So he decided to come home.

Lo and behold, out of the gates of the city came his dear queen-wife, holding in her arms the most perfect, beautiful baby boy he had ever seen.

They went on living as they always had before. But the boy grew. He grew fast! Not by the count of days, but by the swift passage of hours. Soon he was a big, strapping lad. What was the king to do? Everyone knows that you must not break a promise to an underwater king.

So one day he took his son, who of course was named Ivan, on a little hike. They walked and walked until they happened upon a perfectly beautiful lake.

The king said, "Ivanushka, I seem to have lost my ring. As you know, I have very important business to think about. Would you mind finding the ring for me? I will be right over there, thinking about my very important business."

Now Ivanushka was a little peeved. Who can find a golden ring in the heart of a forest? It probably fell into the water. Still, he searched and searched. Before long, an old woman, quite bent over and not a little frightening, came up to him.

She said, "Prince Ivan, is there anything I can do to help you?"

"Get out of my face, you stupid old hag! Can't you see that I'm busy?" he grumbled.

"Well, if it's going to be like that, have a nice day."

She hobbled away.

But Ivan felt badly about the way he'd spoken to the old woman, and he began to reproach himself. After all, old people are wise, and perhaps the woman could have told him something useful.

So he caught up with her and said, "I'm sorry, I don't know what came over me. I am looking for a golden ring, and I am in a bad mood. Please forgive me."

"Ah, Ivanushka, you are looking for a ring that doesn't exist! Your father left you here. You see, he made a promise to the king who lives at the bottom of the waters. He is, in fact, the king of Underland. Your father has promised you to this king."

Like all good princes named Ivan, the poor boy found a log to sit on and began to cry.

"Do not cry, Ivanushka!" the old woman said. "I will tell you what you must do. Now look over there—do you see that nice big currant bush? No, don't eat the berries! Hide behind it! In a little while, you will see twelve beautiful doves flying down. When they hit Mother Earth, they will turn into beautiful maidens who will go into the lake and swim. Do nothing, but wait for the thirteenth dove who will fly down after them. She will also hit Mother Earth and turn into a beautiful maiden. As soon as she goes into the water, grab her shirt and hide it. When she comes looking for it, give it back to her, but not before she gives you her golden ring. If she does not do this, all is lost!"

Ivanushka thanked the old woman and dutifully hid behind the currant bush. The berries were very red and smelled very sweet, and he very much wanted to eat them. However, Prince Ivan was no fool, and he waited as the old woman had instructed him.

After a while, twelve doves flew down, hit Mother Earth, and turned into twelve beautiful maidens who threw off their shirts, jumped into the water, and started to play. Ivan waited, and a thirteenth dove came. She was as pure white as a spring morning. When she hit Mother Earth, she turned into the most beautiful woman Ivan had ever seen. She also tossed off her white linen shirt and jumped into the water to play with her sisters. Ivan sat there and stared. She was so beautiful that he could not take his eyes off her!

Soon, they started to come up out of the water again, and Ivan remembered what he must do. Quickly, he jumped out, took the shirt, and hid before anyone saw him.

The twelve sisters put on their shirts, but the thirteenth could not find hers. The sisters looked under the trees and behind the bushes, but they could find nothing.

Finally the thirteenth sister said, "O my sisters, it is my fault. I should have been more careful. You go, and I will take care of this."

So the twelve girls hit Mother Earth, turned into beautiful doves, and flew away.

Now the thirteenth sister said, "Whoever stole my shirt, please give it back to me. If you are an old man, you will be like a father to me. If you are a -middle-aged man, you will be like an older brother to me. If you are a young man, you will be my dearest friend."

So Ivanushka crept from behind the currant bush and gave her the shirt.

She said, "Ivanushka, where have you been?" She gave him her golden ring and said, "My father, the king of Underland, is very angry with you. But don't worry. I will help you. You are a great friend to me now. This is what you must do: go down into the water. You won't drown, just keep walking down. Then announce yourself to the king, and do whatever he says."

After this, she hit Mother Earth, turned into the most beautiful white dove he had ever seen, and flew away.

As I have said, Ivanushka was no fool. So he did as the girl had instructed. Though he was terribly frightened, he jumped into the water and swam. The water surrounded him on all sides, but he found he could breathe easily enough. He swam on and on until he reached the kingdom of Underland. To his surprise, it was just like his own kingdom! There were forests and fields, palaces and buildings. Ahead of him was the palace of the king.

Ivan marched right in and went directly to the throne room. The king was there, sitting on his throne with the most stormy aspect Ivan had ever seen.

"Where have you been?" the king growled. "I am quite cross with you. So, here is what you will do: I have a piece of land just behind my palace. It is thirty miles wide and thirty miles long, and it is covered with trees, ditches, and boulders. Over the course of this single night, you must clear it all out until it is as smooth as my palm. And then, during this same night, you will sow the field with white wheat. That wheat will grow so high that a red-winged blackbird will be able to hide inside the field of wheat. If you cannot do this, I will take off your head."

Ivan left the throne room and went outside. He wept, and he wept some more. Then he saw, leaning out of a nearby parapet, the thirteenth daughter. Her name was Vasilissa the Wise.

She leaned over the parapet and said, "Ivanushka, why are you crying?"

"How can I not cry? Your father has given me an impossible task! I am supposed to clear that field behind your palace that is thirty miles wide and thirty miles long, filled with trees, ditches, and boulders the size of houses. How will I ever do this? He told me that he would take my head off my shoulders if I do not do this by morning!"

"That is not any kind of trouble," she said. "The real trouble is yet to come. Go to sleep, Ivanushka. The morning is wiser than the evening."

Ivanushka, dutiful as always, went straight to sleep.

But Vasilissa cried, "Wake up, my dear friends and neighbors! Clear out that field! Sow it with the most beautiful wheat, and ensure it grows so high that a red-winged blackbird can hide in it."

The next morning, Ivanushka woke up, got out of bed, and went outside. Lo and behold, the field was as smooth as the king's palm. White wheat grew as high as his head so that a whole flock of red-winged blackbirds could hide in it.

Ivanushka went to the king and said, "It is done!"

The king was quite impressed.

He said, "Well! You are a good servant. Very good! I will give you another task. I have three hundred granaries filled with wheat. You have one night to clean it all out and pile the grain up in neat stacks without a single bit of chaff. And you know that if you cannot do this, I will simply have to take off your head."

Ivanushka walked outside and started to weep. And there was Vasilissa the Wise once again, leaning over the parapet.

"Ivanushka," she called. "Why are you weeping?"

"Vasilissa," he said, "it is impossible! Your father the king wants me to clean three hundred granaries' worth of wheat, and if I do not do this by tomorrow morning, he will take off my head!"

"Ah, Ivanushka," she said. "That is not any sort of trouble. The real trouble is still to come. Go to bed. The morning is wiser than the evening."

Ivanushka did as she said.

Vasilissa cried out, "Come to me, all my dear ants! Clear out all of the wheat in the granaries and pile them up perfectly!"

The ants went to work.

When Ivanushka awoke, he went to the granaries. Lo and behold, they were piled with perfectly cleaned wheat.

Ivanushka ran to the king and said, "Sire, it is done!"

The king said, "Well, well! I am very impressed. However, I have a final task for you. This night, you must build for me an entire church out of wax. If you do not do this, your head is mine."

Ivanushka walked out of the throne room, and my, did he weep! Vasilissa was there again too, leaning over the parapet. On her face was a mysterious smile.

"Ivanushka, why are you crying?"

"How can I not cry!" he said. "Your father told me to build an entire church of nothing but wax! If I cannot do it, he will have my head!"

"Ah Ivanushka," she said. "This is no trouble at all. The real trouble is still to come. Go to bed. The morning is wiser than the evening."

Ivanushka did as she said.

Vasilissa cried out, "Oh my dear, work-loving bees, come to me from all the corners of the earth! Build for me the most beautiful church entirely of wax!"

When Ivanushka awoke, he was sure that this would be the day of his death. Yet when he looked out the window, he saw a beautiful church made entirely of wax.

Before the sun came out to melt it, he ran to the throne room and said, "Sire, it is done!"

"I am quite impressed with you," said the king. "Come, I have thirteen daughters. Choose any one of them to be your wife. You are a worthy son to me."

Well, as you can guess, Ivanushka did not take long to decide. He chose Vasilissa, and they lived happily for some time in Underland.

But soon Ivanushka started to grow restless. One day, Vasilissa saw him walking around downcast and depressed.

Vasilissa said, "Ivanushka, what is wrong?"

"I miss my father, I miss my mother, and I miss holy Rus!" he replied. "I want to go home."

Vasilissa looked at him and said, "Ah, this is the great trouble we have all been waiting for. The king will not let you go. We must escape. If we try, the king will not rest until he catches us. But I will help you."

She turned around, spat in three corners of the room, gathered all her things, and took two of the best horses her father had. Then they escaped, as fast as possible, out of Underland to holy Rus.

When it was early morning, the servant came knocking at their door.

"Lovebirds!" she called. "It's time to get up! The king is awaiting your presence."

One of the drops of spit said, "Just a little more time. We're so tired!"

So the servant went away.

Two hours later, she came back, pounded on the door, and said, "Lovebirds, it is time to get up! The king is starting to get annoyed!"

The second drop of spit piped up: "We're getting up, don't worry! It's just taking us a little longer than usual."

Two hours later, the servant came back with two burly guards who started to pound the door angrily.

"Get up!" she called. "The king is angry! He is about to have our heads!"

The third drop of spit said, "We're putting on our clothes —any minute now!"

This time, the servants did not leave. They waited, and they waited. Finally, they broke down the door. Lo and behold, no one was there! They went and told the king, and the king was furious.

"Go, find them! Bring them back!" he said.

And the servants went. Meanwhile, Ivanushka and Vasilissa were riding as fast as they could. But Vasilissa had a nagging sense that everything was not as it should be.

She said, "Ivanushka, stop. Lie down on Mother Earth. Put your ear to the ground and tell me what you hear."

Ivanushka did.

He said, "I hear the loud conversation of men and the pounding of horses' hooves."

"They are coming for us!" she said.

So she transformed the horses into a meadow, herself into a sheep, and Ivanushka into an old, decrepit shepherd. Just in time! There, the servants of the king rode up.

Seeing the shepherd, they said, "Old man, have you seen a young prince and princess riding horses?"

The shepherd said, "I've been living here for forty years, and I've never seen a horse in my life."

The riders, not being very bright, said, "Sorry to bother you."

Returning to the king, they declared, "We found nothing. All we saw was a green field, a sheep, and a shepherd."

"You idiots!" said the king. "That was Vasilissa and Ivan! Go back, find them!"

So they did. In the meantime, Ivanushka and Vasilissa rode and rode. Vasilissa again had a sense that something was wrong.

She said, "Ivanushka, stop. Lie down on Mother Earth. Put your ear to the ground and tell me what you hear."

Ivanushka did.

He said, "I hear the loud conversation of men and the pounding of horses' hooves."

"They are coming for us!" she said.

So she transformed herself into a church, him into an old priest, and the horses into trees. The servants came riding up. Seeing the priest, they thought, *He is a priest. He will tell us the truth.*

They said, "Old priest, have you seen a shepherd and a sheep?"

The priest said, "I've served here for forty years. I've never seen a sheep in my life."

The servants didn't know what to do, so they rode back

and told the king that they had seen a priest and a church but that the priest had not seen either a sheep or a shepherd.

"You idiots!" cried the king. "That was them!"

This time, the king saddled his own horse, sat on it, and rode like the wind. In the meantime, Ivanushka and Vasilissa had come right to the edge of holy Rus. But Vasilissa had a sense that all was not as it should be.

She said, "Ivanushka, stop. Lie down on Mother Earth. Put your ear to the ground and tell me what you hear."

Ivanushka did.

He said, "I hear the loud conversation of men and the loudest, fastest horse I have ever heard!"

"This is the great trouble we have waited for!" Vasilissa said.

So she transformed the horses into a lake, herself into a duck, and him into a drake. The king of Underland rode up. He saw, and he knew it was them. He turned himself into a great eagle. He flew up, then came down on the duck with talons outstretched!

The duck went down into the water, and the eagle could not catch it. He flew back up and charged the drake. But the drake went down into the water, and the eagle could not catch it. So the eagle flew back up again, spread his wings, and dove as fast as he could. Both the duck and the drake went down into the water.

Up and down they went until the king was utterly exhausted and no longer able to hold the shape of the eagle.

Falling down next to his horse, he said, "Go! I have no more time for you."

The king rode away. Ivanushka and Vasilissa the Wise rode up to the palace of Ivan's parents. There they dismounted, and Ivanushka stopped Vasilissa in a little glade.

He said, "I want to tell my parents about you before you meet them. Wait here for me."

Vasilissa looked long and hard at him and said, "Ivanushka, you're going to forget me."

"Me forget you? Are you crazy? I'll never forget you! Just wait. I will go, hug them, tell them about you, and bring you back."

She looked long and hard at him and said, "Remember me when you see two doves hitting a window."

"Don't be ridiculous!" he said.

Ivanushka went. His parents ran out of the castle and hugged him. They were so overjoyed that Ivanushka forgot all about Vasilissa. He and his parents feasted for days and days. Finally, Ivanushka began to think it might be time for him to get married.

In the meantime, Vasilissa walked into the village and took a job at a bakery. She was very good at baking—so good that the whole village started to come to eat there and buy her bread.

One morning, Vasilissa woke up and told the baker, "I am going to make some doves out of dough."

She made two beautiful doves, put them into the oven, and asked the baker, "What do you think those doves are going to do when they are finished baking?"

He said, "I know what they're going to do—they're going to fly into my mouth, and I will eat them!"

She replied, "That is not what they are going to do."

When she opened the oven, out flew two beautiful doves. They flew straight out of the bakery and to the palace, where they beat at the window with all their strength, as though they were trying to get in. Ivanushka happened to be passing by that window, and when he saw the doves, he remembered Vasilissa.

"Oh my goodness!" he said. "What have I been doing?"

He ran to the baker's, took her in his arms, kissed her, and took her to his parents, who welcomed her as their own daughter. They lived there together for many happy years.

EPILOGUE

As a short epilogue to this special collection of Slavic fairy tales, I want to offer a word from one of my favorite thinkers—the Russian philosopher Ivan Ilyin. It is an entirely avoidable tragedy that his name has been associated, I believe unfairly, with the excesses of the current Russian political regime. There is not enough in English (yet) to prove to you, my readers, the worth of this man's thinking and writing.

So you'll have to take a leap of faith, and I hope you will, until I am able to translate and share more of his work with the English-speaking world. I will let his words speak for him, but let me simply say one more thing. Consider that this wondrous and positive vision of humanity was written in a world when actual Nazis had come dangerously close to the sort of domination that would have changed the course of history in an unspeakable direction. Ilyin himself was an exile from his home, having no hope of returning in his lifetime. And yet, he believed that the modern world is on the path to spiritual renewal!

This is the same man who told an auditorium full of educated noblemen that they should read fairy tales, because in fairy tales they would find the keys to renewing their own spiritual and intellectual lives. This is why I end this collection with this short essay, which Ilyin wrote to his wife "in creative spiritual union." Do not be put off by his reference to "philosophy" as a saving activity. Remember that in Ilyin's mind, a philosopher—that is, a lover of wisdom—is first and foremost a lover of story. Please share his words, his vision, with others.

~

Renewed Humanity
Professor Ivan Ilyin
(to his wife, in creative spiritual union)

The modern world is on the path to spiritual renewal. Perhaps some do not yet see this because this epoch, truly, is tragic beyond measure, and many find their spirits entirely quenched. Others, perhaps, have felt the necessity of such renewal, but as yet can see no path to it, and do not know where to put their trust. However, this renewal will inevitably begin, it will begin seemingly on its own, and exactly at the moment when human suffering seems no longer endurable.

This is why it is so important for us to overcome the inexorable march of history and come to know what must be done. After all, it is unworthy of humanity to simply float along the current of fate. It is important to anticipate our fate and to work at perfecting it. How many trials, troubles, or calamities the Almighty has sent us to awaken us, to bring us back to ourselves, to help us remember that we are free creators, to reveal within ourselves the profound depths of our spiritual existence, and to begin, from those depths, our own renewal willingly, bravely, and insistently!

Let us think, first of all, about what we have lost. Mankind tried to create a culture without faith, without heart, without contemplation, and without conscience, and now we are faced with the obviousness of its collapse. People no longer wanted to believe, because they had convinced themselves that faith is something contrary to reason, unscientific, and reactionary. They rejected also the heart, because the heart seemed to them a hindrance to instinct, something foolish, sentimental, depriving man of necessary efficiency, while a smart person instead must seek to remain an egotist and a "doer." They also rejected contemplation, because their cold mind sweeps away "fruitless fantasy," considering the prosaic to be the most important thing in life. They also left no room for conscience within themselves, because its living commands do not fit in the context of calculating resourcefulness. Behind all this hides a false shame at appearing to be poor and unnoticed, childish and ridiculous. This is nothing but unfulfilled vanity and fear before "public opinion."

This false shame will be overcome by the great sufferings of our age, for suffering is true reality, it is existence itself, it is so real that people forget about their desire to *appear* to be anything at all. But this also means that we will have to suffer for a long time still, perhaps in even worse and heretofore unimagined forms of humiliation and oppression, and to continue to endure until everything "seeming," conditional, and dead fades away inside us, and until the source of inner reality and creative power triumphantly breaks out. We must once again feel the essential need of true reality, the essence of being and life. Only then will our souls come alive; only then will we freely and decisively give ourselves over to the contemplation of the heart. Having, moreover, found God again, will we make peace with our conscience and begin to create a new culture, a new faith, a new science, and new art, a new rule of law, and a new society.

When exactly this understanding will come and when this creative breakthrough will occur is difficult to predict. But we must, even now, by all possible means and from all possible points of view, try to correctly diagnose this current spiritual crisis and and to feel out, in the darkness, the true paths for future renewal.

Philosophy especially is called to this, for it is love of wisdom, it is creative need of divine content, as a will toward necessary actions that are both central and marginal. Philosophy will do what is right if it dedicates itself to this task.

Then, philosophy will be able to see, first of all, the spiritual wounds of contemporary culture, and, having begun an examination of the reasons for the defilement of the sacred things of life, will look into the very abyss of evil.

After that, philosophy will have to spiritually diagnose our crisis, the better to show to what degree contemporary humanity overvalues the life of the senses, how it calls to life a heartless culture and plunges into the chaos of earthly darkness.

Having directed its gaze to the paths of spiritual renewal, philosophy will have to turn first of all to the problem of education, in order to show its most important goals, most neglected by this modern age, including awakening the spiritual instinct in childhood, strengthening the child's own objective power of discernment and will to spiritual wholeness.

We must give an accurate assessment of the difficulties of earthly existence, which we must bear on our own shoulders, and we must find natural and virtuous paths to lessen them in a social setting.

It is extremely important to understand and fully appreciate the essence of the creative life of people. This is the great project for future generations. The structure of the cultural act should be renewed to its very depths and from those very depths, and this must be done in all aspects of our activity, in all the regions of the spirit.

To achieve this, we must once again stand on the path of the first principles of life: to learn once again to value freedom, to allow good to flourish within ourselves, to be imbued with humility, which gives strength, to bow before the divine mystery of the world, to abandon ourselves to accidental contemplation, to learn the joy of thanksgiving and through this, in true religiosity, to find the fountainhead of life itself.

Only then will spiritual renewal radiate into the world, illumining its entire life, leading culture toward true Christianity.

ALSO BY NICHOLAS KOTAR

The Raven Son Series

The Song of the Sirin

The Curse of the Raven

The Heart of the World

The Forge of the Covenant

The Throne of the Gods

The Worldbuilding Series:

How to Survive a Russian Fairy Tale

Heroes for All Times

A Window to the Russian Soul

ABOUT THE AUTHOR

Nicholas Kotar is a writer of epic fantasy inspired by Russian fairy tales, a freelance translator from Russian to English, the resident conductor of the men's choir at a Russian monastery in the middle of nowhere, and a semi-professional vocalist. His one great regret in life is that he was not born in the nineteenth century in St. Petersburg, but he is doing everything he can to remedy that error.

9 781951 536305